For Ernestine
Joanna

# minedition

English edition published 2017 by Michael Neugebauer Publishing Ltd., Hong Kong

Text copyright © 2017 Géraldine Elschner
Illustration copyright © 2017 Joanna Boillat
Rights arranged with "minedition" Rights and Licensing AG, Zurich, Switzerland.

Michael Neugebauer Publishing Ltd., Unit 28, 5/F, Metro Centre, Phase 2,
No.21 Lam Hing Street, Kowloon Bay, Kowloon, Hong Kong.
Phone +852 2807 1711, e-mail: info@minedition.com

This edition was printed in May 2017
at L.Rex Printing Co Ltd.
3/F., Blue Box Factory Building, 25 Hing Wo
Street, Tin Wan, Aberdeen, Hong Kong, China
Typesetting in Bauhaus
Library of Congress Cataloging-in-Publication
Data available upon request.

ISBN 978-988-8341-43-6
10 9 8 7 6 5 4 3 2 1 First Impression

For more information please visit our website:
www.minedition.com

# Pompon

by Géraldine Elschner

with pictures by Joanna Boillat

minedition

Pompon was a simple white bear who lived in the museum. Actually, he was just a statue of a white bear, and he felt like he would never travel anywhere.

It was an ordinary day for Pompon—a gloomy, gray morning with nothing to do and no one to play with. But today would be the day someone gave Pompon wings.

At around ten o'clock, a small boy named Leo came along.

Leo stopped in front of Pompon's nose and
stood on his toes to look up at him.

For a long time he stared into Pompon's eyes,
which were as deep as the sea.

Once, twice, three times Leo ran around the
white base on which the white bear stood.

For a long time he studied the arch of Pompon's legs, which were as tall as a gate.

For a long time he imagined sliding down Pompon's back, as if on a sled.

Leo observed the curve of Pompon's ear, which looked like an igloo.
His eyes settled on Pompon's fur, which was as smooth and white
as snow.

Though he was made of stone, Pompon seemed to stand as proudly as a peacock.

Pompon had to admit this was the best part of living in a museum. He liked to be admired.

Leo, however, had a special look in
his eyes—a magical look.
He stretched out his hand, and with
a sweet smile...

he stroked Pompon's white cheek.

**Caution!**
Please do not touch the statues.
Even clean skin contains oils
which will harm the artwork.

"STOP!" bellowed
a voice. It was the
museum guard.
"It's forbidden to touch
the art!" he said sternly.

Leo winced.
"I'm sorry," he said, "but... but..."

"But WHAT?" the guard shouted.

Leo lowered his head.
"I couldn't resist," he said softly.

The guard's fury seemed to melt.
"I know... I know..." he said in a wistful
manner, as if he'd once been in Leo's
shoes himself. "Please just don't do it
again, promise?"

"I promise," Leo said.

But...

Pompon's transformation had already begun.
A single touch from a curious boy had been
enough.

A barely noticeable shudder ran along the length
of Pompon's back. He felt as if someone had
given him wings.

When night came,
after all the guests had
gone, and while Leo was
at home in his bed, wondering what the
museum guards might be up to that evening,
something mysterious happened...

Pompon flew away.

He journeyed farther than he ever imagined,
on the wings an admirer had given him.
Where did he go? In which country
does he live, or in which sky?
Did he become a pelican or
a swan? Perhaps a dove—
or something altogether
different. Nobody knows.

But ever since that magical day
it is Pompon's twin brother
who stands in his place at the
museum, on that same white base
where Pompon used to live.

And he is waiting for someone
like you to visit him.

In the gardens of a small commune in Saulieu, France, a large white bear prowls between the thickets. Just to look at him, you would think he moves!

In 1922 when the white bear now affectionately known as "Pompon" arrived at the Salon de Paris, the enormous statue (measuring nearly seven feet long)—with his smooth, striking shape carved of stone—immediately made its creator famous.

Sculptor François Pompon (1855-1933) was a small mustachioed man who, in addition to being one of the most sought-after sculpture assistants in France, worked for much of his life on the animals he loved. At the Jardin des Plantes in Paris he spent his Sundays modeling clay as his menagerie of creations grew. His signature style included few details, but simplified the animal shapes down to clean lines and pure forms that were at once engaging. He created a whole bestiary of wonderful creatures—turtledoves, owls, bulls, ducks, and panthers, not to mention his most famous white bear.

Grande Bacchante

Young girl with jug, or Water carrier

A discovery at Pompeii

White bear

Joseph Bernard
(1866 – 1931)

Joseph Bernard
(1866 – 1931)

François Pompon
(1855 – 1933)

Julien Moulin
(1832 – 1884)